Sir Thomas Malory

The Death of King Arthur

PENGUIN BOOKS

PENGUIN BOOKS

Published by the Penguin Group
Penguin Books Ltd, 27 Wrights Lane, London w8 5tz, England
Penguin Books USA Inc., 375 Hudson Street, New York, New York, 10014, USA
Penguin Books Australia Ltd, Ringwood, Victoria, Australia
Penguin Books Canada Ltd, 10 Alcorn Avenue, Toronto, Ontario, Canada m4v 3b2
Penguin Books (NZ) Ltd, 182–190 Wairau Road, Auckland 10, New Zealand

Penguin Books Ltd, Registered Offices: Harmondsworth, Middlesex, England

This extract is from *Le Morte d'Arthur* by Sir Thomas Malory, published in
Penguin Classics 1969
This edition published 1995
1 3 5 7 9 10 8 6 4 2

Filmset by Datix International Limited, Bungay, Suffolk
Printed in England by Clays Ltd, St Ives plc

Chapter 1

HOW SIR MORDRED PRESUMED AND TOOK ON HIM TO BE KING OF ENGLAND, AND WOULD HAVE MARRIED THE QUEEN, HIS FATHER'S WIFE

As Sir Mordred was ruler of all England, he did do make letters as though that they came from beyond the sea, and the letters specified that King Arthur was slain in battle with Sir Launcelot. Wherefore Sir Mordred made a parliament, and called the lords together, and there he made them to choose him king; and so was he crowned at Canterbury, and held a feast there fifteen days; and afterward he drew him unto Winchester, and there he took the queen Guenever, and said plainly that he would wed her which was his uncle's wife and his father's wife. And so he made ready for the feast, and a day prefixed that they should be wedded; wherefore Queen Guenever was passing heavy. But she durst not discover her heart, but spake fair, and agreed to Sir Mordred's will.

Then she desired of Sir Mordred for to go to London, to buy all manner of things that longed unto the wedding. And because of her fair speech Sir Mordred trusted her well enough, and gave her leave to go. And so when she came to London she took the Tower of London, and suddenly in all haste possible she stuffed it with all manner of victual, and well garnished it with men, and so kept it.

Then when Sir Mordred wist and understood how he was beguiled, he was passing wroth out of measure. And a short tale for to make, he went and laid a mighty siege about the Tower of London, and made many great assaults thereat, and threw many great engines unto them, and shot great guns. But all might not prevail Sir Mordred, for Queen Guenever would never for fair speech nor for foul, would never trust to come in his hand again.

Then came the Bishop of Canterbury, the which was a noble clerk and an holy man, and thus he said to Sir Mordred: 'Sir, what will do? Will ye first displease God and sithen shame yourself, and all knighthood? Is not King Arthur your uncle, no farther but your mother's brother, and on her himself King Arthur begat you, upon his own sister, therefore how may you wed your father's wife? Sir,' said the noble clerk, 'leave this opinion or I shall curse you with book and bell and candle.'

'Do thou thy worst,' said Sir Mordred, 'wit thou well I shall defy thee.'

'Sir,' said the Bishop, 'and wit you well I shall not fear me to do that me ought to do. Also where ye noise where my lord Arthur is slain, and that is not so, and therefore ye will make a foul work in this land.'

'Peace, thou false priest,' said Sir Mordred, 'for and thou chafe me any more I shall make strike off thy head.'

So the Bishop departed and did the cursing in the most orgulest wise that might be done. And then Sir Mordred sought the Bishop of Canterbury, for to have slain him. Then the Bishop fled, and took part of his goods with him, and went nigh unto Glastonbury; and there he was as priest hermit in a chapel, and lived in poverty and in holy prayers, for well he understood that mischievous war was at hand.

Then Sir Mordred sought on Queen Guenever by letters and sondes, and by fair means and foul means, for to have her to come out of the Tower of London; but all this availed not, for she answered him shortly, openly and privily, that she had lever slay herself than to be married with him.

Then came word to Sir Mordred that King Arthur had araised the siege for Sir Launcelot, and he was coming homeward with a great host, to be avenged upon Sir Mordred; wherefore Sir Mordred made write writs to all the barony of this land, and much people drew to him. For then was the common voice among them that with Arthur was none other life but war and strife, and with Sir Mordred was great joy and bliss. Thus was Sir Arthur depraved, and evil said of. And many there were that King Arthur had made up of nought, and given them lands, might not then say him a good word.

Lo ye all Englishmen, see ye not what a mischief here was? For he that was the most king and knight of the world, and most loved the fellowship of noble knights, and by him they were all upholden, now might not these Englishmen hold them content with him. Lo thus was the old custom and usage of this land; and also men say that we of this land have not yet lost ne forgotten that custom and usage. Alas, this is a great default of us Englishmen, for there may nothing please us no term.

And so fared the people at that time, they were better pleased with Sir Mordred than they were with King Arthur; and much people drew unto Sir Mordred, and said they would abide with him for better and for worse. And so Sir Mordred drew with a great host to Dover, for there he heard say that Sir Arthur would arrive, and so he thought to beat his own father from his lands; and the most part of all England held with Sir Mordred, the people were so new fangle.

Chapter 2

HOW AFTER THAT KING ARTHUR HAD TIDINGS,
HE RETURNED AND CAME TO DOVER, WHERE
SIR MORDRED MET HIM TO LET HIS LANDING;
AND OF THE DEATH OF SIR GAWAIN

And so as Sir Mordred was at Dover with his host, there came King Arthur with a great navy of ships, and galleys, and carracks. And there was Sir Mordred ready awaiting upon his landage, to let his own father to land up the land that he was king over.

Then there was launching of great boats and small, and full of noble men of arms; and there was much slaughter of gentle knights, and many a full bold baron was laid full low, on both parties.

But King Arthur was so courageous that there might no manner of knights let him to land, and his knights fiercely followed him; and so they landed maugre Sir Mordred's and all his power, and put Sir Mordred aback, that he fled and all his people.

So when this battle was done, King Arthur let bury his people that were dead. And then was noble Sir Gawain found in a great boat, lying more than half dead. When Sir Arthur wist that Sir Gawain was laid so low, he went unto him; and there the king made sorrow out of measure, and took Sir Gawain in his arms, and thrice he there swooned.

And then when he awaked, he said, 'Alas, Sir

Gawain, my sister's son, here now thou liest, the man in the world that I loved most; and now is my joy gone, for now, my nephew Sir Gawain, I will discover me unto your person: in Sir Launcelot and you I most had my joy, and mine affiance, and now have I lost my joy of you both; wherefore all mine earthly joy is gone from me.'

'Mine uncle King Arthur,' said Sir Gawain, 'wit you well my death day is come, and all is through mine own hastiness and wilfulness; for I am smitten upon the old wound the which Sir Launcelot gave me, on the which I feel well I must die; and had Sir Launcelot been with you as he was, this unhappy war had never begun; and of all this am I causer, for Sir Launcelot and his blood, through their prowess, held all your cankered enemies in subjection and danger. And now,' said Sir Gawain, 'ye shall miss Sir Launcelot. But alas, I would not accord with him, and therefore,' said Sir Gawain, 'I pray you, fair uncle, that I may have paper, pen and ink, that I may write to Sir Launcelot a cedle with mine own hands.'

And then when paper and ink was brought, then Gawain was set up weakly by King Arthur, for he was shriven a little tofore; and then he wrote thus, as the French book maketh mention:

'Unto Sir Launcelot, flower of all noble knights that ever I heard of or saw by my days, I, Sir Gawain, King Lot's son of Orkney, sister's son unto the noble King Arthur, send thee greeting, and let thee have knowledge that the tenth day of May I was smitten upon the old wound that thou gavest me afore the city of Benwick, and through the same wound that thou gavest me I am come to my death day. And I will that all the world wit, that I, Sir Gawain, knight of the Table Round, sought my death, and not through thy deserving, but it was mine own seeking; wherefore I beseech thee, Sir Launcelot, to return again unto this realm, and see my tomb, and pray some prayer more or less for my soul. And this same day that I wrote this cedle, I was hurt to the death in the same wound, the which I had of thy hand, Sir Launcelot; for of a more nobler man might I not be slain.

'Also Sir Launcelot, for all the love that ever was betwixt us, make no tarrying, but come over the sea in all haste, that thou mayst with thy noble knights rescue that noble king that made thee knight, that is my lord Arthur, for he is full straitly bestad with a false traitor, that is my half-brother, Sir Mordred; and he hath let crown him king, and would have wedded my lady Queen Guenever, and so had he done had she not put herself in the Tower of London. And so the tenth day of May last past, my lord Arthur and we all landed upon them at Dover; and there we put that false traitor, Sir Mordred, to flight, and there it misfortuned me to be stricken upon thy stroke. And at the date of this letter was written, but two hours and a half afore my death, written with mine own hand, and so subscribed with part of my heart's blood. And I require thee, most famous knight of the world, that thou wilt see my tomb.'

And then Sir Gawain wept, and King Arthur wept; and then they swooned both. And when they awaked both, the king made Sir Gawain to receive his Saviour. And then Sir Gawain prayed the king for to send for Sir Launcelot, and to cherish him above all other knights.

And so at the hour of noon Sir Gawain yielded up the spirit; and then the king let inter him in a chapel within Dover Castle; and there yet all men may see the skull of him, and the same wound is seen that Sir Launcelot gave him in battle.

Then was it told the king that Sir Mordred had pitched a new field upon Barham Down. And upon the morn the king rode thither to him, and there was a great battle betwixt them, and much people was slain on both parties; but at the last Sir Arthur's party stood best, and Sir Mordred and his party fled unto Canterbury.

Chapter 3

HOW AFTER, SIR GAWAIN'S GHOST APPEARED TO KING ARTHUR, AND WARNED HIM THAT HE SHOULD NOT FIGHT THAT DAY

And then the king let search all the towns for his knights that were slain, and interred them; and salved them with soft salves that so sore were wounded.

Then much people drew unto King Arthur. And then they said that Sir Mordred warred upon King

Arthur with wrong. And then King Arthur drew him with his host down by the seaside westward toward Salisbury; and there was a day assigned betwixt King Arthur and Sir Mordred, that they should meet upon a down beside Salisbury, and not far from the seaside; and this day was assigned on a Monday after Trinity Sunday, whereof King Arthur was passing glad, that he might be avenged upon Sir Mordred.

Then Sir Mordred araised much people about London, for they of Kent, Sussex and Surrey, Essex, and of Suffolk, and of Norfolk, held the most part with Sir Mordred; and many a full noble knight drew unto Sir Mordred and to the king; but they loved Sir Launcelot drew unto Sir Mordred.

So upon Trinity Sunday at night, King Arthur dreamed a wonderful dream, and that was this: that him seemed he sat upon a chaflet in a chair, and the chair was fast to a wheel, and thereupon sat King Arthur in the richest cloth of gold that might be made; and the king thought there was under him, far from him, an hideous deep black water, and therein were all manner of serpents, and worms, and wild beasts, foul and horrible;

and suddenly the king thought the wheel turned up-so-down, and he fell among the serpents, and every beast took him by a limb; and then the king cried as he lay in his bed and slept, 'Help.'

And then knights, squires, and yeomen, awaked the king; and then he was so amazed that he wist not where he was; and then he fell on slumbering again, not sleeping nor thoroughly waking.

So the king seemed verily that there came Sir Gawain unto him with a number of fair ladies with him. And when King Arthur saw him, then he said, 'Welcome my sister's son; I weened thou hadst been dead, and now I see thee alive, much am I beholding unto Almighty Jesu. O fair nephew and my sister's son, what be these ladies that hither be come with you?'

'Sir,' said Sir Gawain, 'all these be ladies for whom I have foughten when I was man living, and all these are those that I did battle for in righteous quarrel; and God hath given them that grace at their great prayer, because I did battle for them, that they should bring me hither unto you: thus much hath God given me leave, for to warn you of your death; for and ye fight as tomorn with Sir

Mordred, as ye both have assigned, doubt ye not ye must be slain, and the most part of your people on both parties. And for the great grace and goodness that Almighty Jesu hath unto you, and for pity of you, and many more other good men there shall be slain, God hath sent me to you of his special grace, to give you warning that in no wise ye do battle as tomorn, but that ye take a treaty for a month day; and proffer you largely, so as tomorn to be put in a delay. For within a month shall come Sir Launcelot with all his noble knights, and rescue you worshipfully, and slay Sir Mordred, and all that ever will hold with him.'

Then Sir Gawain and all the ladies vanished. And anon the king called upon his knights, squires, and yeomen, and charged them wightly to fetch his noble lords and wise bishops unto him. And when they were come, the king told them his avision, what Sir Gawain had told him, and warned him that if he fought on the morn he should be slain.

Then the king commanded Sir Lucan the Butler, and his brother Sir Bedevere, with two bishops with them, and charged them in any wise, and they might: 'Take a treaty for a month day with Sir

Mordred, and spare not, proffer him lands and goods as much as ye think best.'

So then they departed, and came to Sir Mordred, where he had a grim host of an hundred thousand men. And there they entreated Sir Mordred long time; and at the last Sir Mordred was agreed for to have Cornwall and Kent, by Arthur's days; after, all England, after the days of King Arthur.

Chapter 4

HOW BY MISADVENTURE OF AN ADDER THE BATTLE BEGAN, WHERE MORDRED WAS SLAIN, AND ARTHUR HURT TO THE DEATH

Then were they condescended that King Arthur and Sir Mordred should meet betwixt both their hosts, and every each of them should bring fourteen persons; and they came with this word unto Arthur.

Then said he, 'I am glad that this is done': and so he went into the field.

And when Arthur should depart, he warned all

his host that and they see any sword drawn, 'look ye come on fiercely, and slay that traitor, Sir Mordred, for I in no wise trust him.'

In likewise Sir Mordred warned his host that: 'And ye see any sword drawn, look that ye come on fiercely, and so slay all that ever before you standeth; for in no wise I will not trust for this treaty, for I know well my father will be avenged on me.'

And so they met as their pointment was, and so they were agreed and accorded thoroughly; and wine was fetched, and they drank.

Right soon came an adder out of a little heath bush, and it stung a knight on the foot. And when the knight felt him stungen, he looked down and saw the adder, and then he drew his sword to slay the adder, and thought of none other harm. And when the host on both parties saw that sword drawn, then they blew beams, trumpets, and horns, and shouted grimly. And so both hosts dressed them together.

And King Arthur took his horse, and said, 'Alas this unhappy day!' and so rode to his party. And Sir Mordred in likewise. And never was there seen a more dolefuller battle in no Christian land; for there was but rushing and riding, foining and striking, and many a grim word was there spoken either to other, and many a deadly stroke. But ever King Arthur rode throughout the battle of Sir Mordred many times, and did full nobly as a noble king should, and at all times he fainted never; and Sir Mordred that day put him in devoir, and in great peril. And thus they fought all the long day, and never stinted till the noble knights were laid to the cold earth; and ever they fought still till it was near night, and by that time was there an hundred thousand laid dead upon the down. Then was Arthur wood wroth out of measure, when he saw his people so slain from him.

Then the king looked about him, and then was he ware, of all his host and of all his good knights, were left no more alive but two knights; that one was Sir Lucan the Butler, and his brother Sir Bedevere, and they were full sore wounded.

'Jesu, mercy,' said the king, 'where are all my noble knights becomen? Alas that ever I should see this doleful day, for now,' said Arthur, 'I am come to mine end. But would to God that I wist where were that traitor Sir Mordred, that hath caused all this mischief.'

Then was King Arthur ware where Sir Mordred leaned upon his sword among a great heap of dead men.

'Now give me my spear,' said Arthur unto Sir Lucan, 'for yonder I have espied the traitor that all this woe hath wrought.'

'Sir, let him be,' said Sir Lucan, 'for he is unhappy; and if ye pass this unhappy day ye shall be right well revenged upon him. Good lord, remember ye of your night's dream, and what the spirit of Sir Gawain told you this night, yet God of his great goodness hath preserved you hitherto. Therefore, for God's sake, my lord, leave off by this, for blessed be God ye have won the field, for here we be three alive, and with Sir Mordred is none alive; and if ye leave off now this wicked day of destiny is past.'

'Tide me death, betide me life,' saith the king, 'now I see him yonder alone he shall never escape mine hands, for at a better avail shall I never have him.'

'God speed you well,' said Sir Bedevere.

Then the king gat his spear in both his hands, and ran toward Sir Mordred, crying, 'Traitor, now is thy death day come.'

And when Sir Mordred heard Sir Arthur, he ran until him with his sword drawn in his hand. And there King Arthur smote Sir Mordred under the shield, with a foin of his spear, throughout the body, more than a fathom. And when Sir Mordred felt that he had his death's wound he thrust himself with the might that he had up to the bur of King Arthur's spear. And right so he smote his father Arthur, with his sword holden in both his hands, on the side of the head, that the sword pierced the helmet and the brain pan, and therewithal Sir Mordred fell stark dead to the earth; and the noble Arthur fell in a swoon to the earth and there he swooned ofttimes.

And Sir Lucan the Butler and Sir Bedevere ofttimes heave him up. And so weakly they led him betwixt them both, to a little chapel not far from the seaside. And when the king was there he thought him well eased. Then heard they people cry in the field.

'Now go thou, Sir Lucan,' said the king, 'and do me to wit what betokens that noise in the field.'

So Sir Lucan departed, for he was grievously wounded in many places. And so as he yede, he saw and hearkened by the moonlight, how that pillers and robbers were comen into the field, to pill and to rob many a full noble knight of brooches, and beads, of many a good ring, and of many a rich jewel; and who that were not dead all out, there they slew them for their harness and their riches. When Sir Lucan understood this work, he came to the king as soon as he might, and told him all what he had heard and seen.

'Therefore by my rede,' said Sir Lucan, 'it is best that we bring you to some town.'

'I would it were so,' said the king.

Chapter 5

HOW KING ARTHUR COMMANDED TO CAST HIS
SWORD EXCALIBUR INTO THE WATER, AND HOW
HE WAS DELIVERED TO LADIES IN A BARGE

'But I may not stand, mine head works so. Ah Sir Launcelot,' said King Arthur, 'this day have I sore missed thee: alas, that ever I was against thee, for now have I my death, whereof Sir Gawain me warned in my dream.'

Then Sir Lucan took up the king the one part, and Sir Bedevere the other part, and in the lifting the king swooned; and Sir Lucan fell in a swoon with the lift, that the part of his guts fell out of his body, and therewith the noble knight's heart brast. And when the king awoke, he beheld Sir Lucan, how he lay foaming at the mouth, and part of his guts lay at his feet.

'Alas,' said the king, 'this is to me a full heavy sight, to see this noble duke so die for my sake, for he would have holpen me, that had more need of help than I. Alas, he would not complain him, his heart was so set to help me: now Jesu have mercy upon his soul!'

Then Sir Bedevere wept for the death of his brother.

'Leave this mourning and weeping,' said the king, 'for all this will not avail me, for wit thou well and I might live myself, the death of Sir Lucan would grieve me evermore; but my time hieth fast,' said the king. 'Therefore,' said Arthur unto

Sir Bedevere, 'take thou Excalibur, my good sword, and go with it to yonder water side, and when thou comest there I charge thee throw my sword in that water, and come again and tell me what thou there seest.'

'My lord,' said Bedevere, 'your commandment shall be done, and lightly bring you word again.'

So Sir Bedevere departed, and by the way he beheld that noble sword, that the pommel and the haft was all of precious stones; and then he said to himself, 'If I throw this rich sword in the water, thereof shall never come good, but harm and loss.' And then Sir Bedevere hid Excalibur under a tree.

And so, as soon as he might, he came again unto the king, and said he had been at the water, and had thrown the sword in the water.

'What saw thou there?' said the king.

'Sir,' he said, 'I saw nothing but waves and winds.'

'That is untruly said of thee,' said the king, 'therefore go thou lightly again, and do my commandment; as thou art to me leve and dear, spare not, but throw it in.'

Then Sir Bedevere returned again, and took the

sword in his hand; and then him thought sin and shame to throw away that noble sword, and so eft he hid the sword, and returned again, and told to the king that he had been at the water and done his commandment.

'What saw thou there?' said the king.

'Sir,' he said, 'I saw nothing but the waters wap and waves wan.'

'Ah, traitor untrue,' said King Arthur, 'now hast thou betrayed me twice. Who would have weened that thou that hast been to me so leve and dear, and thou art named a noble knight, and would betray me for the riches of the sword? But now go again lightly, for thy long tarrying putteth me in great jeopardy of my life, for I have taken cold. And but if thou do now as I bid thee, if ever I may see thee, I shall slay thee mine own hands; for thou wouldst for my rich sword see me dead.'

Then Sir Bedevere departed, and went to the sword, and lightly took it up, and went to the water side; and there he bound the girdle about the hilts, and then he threw the sword as far into the water as he might; and there came an arm and an hand above the water and met it, and caught it, and so shook it thrice and brandished, and then vanished away the hand with the sword in the water. So Sir Bedevere came again to the king, and told him what he saw.

'Alas,' said the king, 'help me hence, for I dread me I have tarried over long.'

Then Sir Bedevere took the king upon his back, and so went with him to that water side. And when they were at the water side, even fast by the bank hoved a little barge with many fair ladies in it, and among them all was a queen, and all they had black hoods, and all they wept and shrieked when they saw King Arthur.

'Now put me into the barge,' said the king.

And so he did softly; and there received him three queens with great mourning; and so they set them down, and in one of their laps King Arthur laid his head.

And then that queen said, 'Ah, dear brother, why have ye tarried so long from me? Alas, this wound on your head hath caught over-much cold.'

And so then they rowed from the land, and Sir Bedevere beheld all those ladies go from him.

Then Sir Bedevere cried, 'Ah my lord Arthur,

what shall become of me, now ye go from me and leave me here alone among mine enemies?'

'Comfort thyself,' said the king, 'and do as well as thou mayest, for in me is no trust for to trust in; for I will into the vale of Avilion to heal me of my grievous wound: and if thou hear never more of me, pray for my soul.'

But ever the queens and ladies wept and shrieked, that it was pity to hear. And as soon as Sir Bedevere had lost the sight of the barge, he wept and wailed, and so took the forest; and so he went all that night, and in the morning he was ware betwixt two holts hoar, of a chapel and an hermitage.

Chapter 6

HOW SIR BEDEVERE FOUND HIM ON THE MORN DEAD IN AN HERMITAGE, AND HOW HE ABODE THERE WITH THE HERMIT

Then was Sir Bedevere glad, and thither he went; and when he came into the chapel, he saw where lay an hermit grovelling on all four, there fast by a tomb was new graven. When the hermit saw Sir Bedevere he knew him well, for he was but little tofore Bishop of Canterbury, that Sir Mordred flemed.

'Sir,' said Bedevere, 'what man is there interred that ye pray so fast for?'

'Fair son,' said the hermit, 'I wot not verily, but by deeming. But this night, at midnight, here came a number of ladies, and brought hither a dead corpse, and prayed me to bury him; and here they offered an hundred tapers, and they gave me an hundred bezants.'

'Alas,' said Sir Bedevere, 'that was my lord King Arthur, that here lieth buried in this chapel.'

Then Sir Bedevere swooned; and when he awoke he prayed the hermit he might abide with him still there, to live with fasting and prayers. 'For from hence will I never go,' said Sir Bedevere, 'by my will, but all the days of my life here to pray for my lord Arthur.'

'Ye are welcome to me,' said the hermit, 'for I know you better than ye ween that I do. Ye are the bold Bedevere, and the full noble duke, Sir Lucan the Butler, was your brother.'

Then Sir Bedevere told the hermit all as ye have heard tofore. So there bode Sir Bedevere with the hermit that was tofore Bishop of Canterbury, and there Sir Bedevere put upon him poor clothes, and served the hermit full lowly in fasting and in prayers.

Thus of Arthur I find never more written in books that be authorised, nor more of the very certainty of his death heard I never read, but thus was he led away in a ship wherein were three queens; that one was King Arthur's sister, Queen Morgan le Fay; the other was the Queen of North-gales; the third was the Queen of the Waste Lands. Also there was Nimue, the chief lady of the lake, that had wedded Pelleas the good knight; and this lady had done much for King Arthur, for she would never suffer Sir Pelleas to be in no place where he should be in danger of his life; and so he lived to the uttermost of his days with her in great rest. More of the death of King Arthur could I never find, but that ladies brought him to his burials; and such one was buried there, that the hermit bare witness that sometime was Bishop of Canterbury, but yet the hermit knew not in certain that he was verily the body of King Arthur; for this tale Sir Bedevere, knight of the Table Round, made it to be written.

Chapter 7

OF THE OPINION OF SOME MEN OF THE DEATH OF KING ARTHUR; AND HOW QUEEN GUENEVER MADE HER A NUN IN ALMESBURY

Yet some men say in many parts of England that King Arthur is not dead, but had by the will of Our Lord Jesu into another place; and men say that he shall come again, and he shall win the holy cross. I will not say that it shall be so, but rather I will say, here in this world he changed his life. But many men say that there is written upon his tomb this verse: HIC IACET ARTHURUS, REX QUONDAM REXQUE FUTURUS.

Thus leave I here Sir Bedevere with the hermit, that dwelled that time in a chapel beside Glastonbury, and there was his hermitage. And so they lived in their prayers, and fastings, and great abstinence.

And when Queen Guenever understood that King Arthur was slain, and all the noble knights, Sir Mordred and all the remnant, then the queen stole away, and five ladies with her, and so she went to Almesbury; and there she let make herself a nun, and ware white clothes and black, and great penance she took, as ever did sinful lady in this land, and never creature could make her merry; but lived in fasting, prayers, and alms-deeds, that all manner of people marvelled how virtuously she was changed.

Now leave we Queen Guenever in Almesbury, a nun in white clothes and black, and there she was abbess and ruler as reason would; and turn we from her, and speak we of Sir Launcelot du Lake.

Chapter 8

HOW WHEN SIR LAUNCELOT HEARD OF THE DEATH OF KING ARTHUR, AND OF SIR GAWAIN, AND OTHER MATTERS, [HE] CAME INTO ENGLAND

And when he heard in his country that Sir Mordred was crowned king in England, and made war against King Arthur, his own father, and would let him to land in his own land, also it was told Sir Launcelot how that Sir Mordred had laid siege about the Tower of London, because the queen would not wed him, then was Sir Launcelot wroth out of measure, and said to his kinsmen,

'Alas, that double traitor Sir Mordred, now me repenteth that ever he escaped my hands, for much shame hath he done unto my lord Arthur; for all I feel by the doleful letter that my lord Sir Gawain sent me, on whose soul Jesu have mercy, that my lord Arthur is full hard bestad. Alas,' said Sir Launcelot, 'that ever I should live to hear that most noble king that made me knight thus to be overset with his subject in his own realm. And this doleful letter that my lord, Sir Gawain, hath sent me afore his death, praying me to see his tomb, wit you well his doleful words shall never go from mine heart, for he was a full noble knight as ever was born; and in an unhappy hour was I born that ever I should have that unhap to slay first Sir Gawain, Sir Gaheris the good knight, and mine own friend Sir Gareth, that full noble knight. Alas, I may say I am unhappy,' said Sir Launcelot, 'that ever I should do thus unhappily, and, alas, yet might I never have hap to slay that traitor, Sir Mordred.'

'Leave your complaints,' said Sir Bors, 'and first revenge you of the death of Sir Gawain; and it will be well done that ye see Sir Gawain's tomb, and secondly that ye revenge my lord Arthur, and my lady, Queen Guenever.'

'I thank you,' said Sir Launcelot, 'for ever ye will my worship.'

Then they made them ready in all the haste that might be, with ships and galleys, with Sir Launcelot and his host to pass into England. And so he passed over the sea till he came to Dover, and there he landed with seven kings, and the number was hideous to behold.

Then Sir Launcelot spered of men of Dover where was King Arthur become. Then the people told him how that he was slain, and Sir Mordred and an hundred thousand died on a day; and how Sir Mordred gave King Arthur there the first battle at his landing, and there was good Sir Gawain slain; and on the morn Sir Mordred fought with the king upon Barham Down, and there the king put Sir Mordred to the worse.

'Alas,' said Sir Launcelot, 'this is the heaviest tidings that ever came to me. Now, fair sirs,' said Sir Launcelot, 'show me the tomb of Sir Gawain.'

And then certain people of the town brought him into the Castle of Dover, and showed him the tomb. Then Sir Launcelot kneeled down and wept, and prayed heartily for his soul. And that night he made a dole, and all they that would come had as much flesh, fish, wine and ale, and every man and woman had twelve pence, come who would. Thus with his own hand dealt he this money, in a mourning gown; and ever he went, and prayed them to pray for the soul of Sir Gawain. And on the morn all the priests and clerks that might be gotten in the country were there, and sang mass of requiem; and there offered first Sir Launcelot, and he offered an hundred pound; and then the seven kings offered forty pound apiece; and also there was a thousand knights, and each of them offered a pound; and the offering dured from morn till night, and Sir Launcelot lay two nights on his tomb in prayers and weeping. Then on the third day Sir Launcelot called the kings, dukes, earls, barons, and knights, and said thus:

'My fair lords, I thank you all of your coming into this country with me, but we came too late, and that shall repent me while I live, but against death may no man rebel. But sithen it is so,' said Sir Launcelot, 'I will myself ride and seek my lady, Queen Guenever, for as I hear say she hath had great pain and much disease; and I heard say that she is fled into the west. Therefore ye all shall abide me here, and but if I come again within fifteen days, then take your ships and your fellowship, and depart into your country, for I will do as I say to you.'

Chapter 9

HOW SIR LAUNCELOT DEPARTED TO SEEK THE QUEEN GUENEVER, AND HOW HE FOUND HER AT ALMESBURY

Then came Sir Bors de Ganis, and said, 'My lord Sir Launcelot, what think ye for to do, now to ride in this realm? Wit ye well ye shall find few friends.'

'Be as be may,' said Sir Launcelot, 'keep you still here, for I will forth on my journey, and no man nor child shall go with me.'

So it was no boot to strive, but he departed and rode westerly, and there he sought a seven or eight days; and at the last he came to a nunnery, and then was Queen Guenever ware of Sir Launcelot as he walked in the cloister. And when she saw him there she swooned thrice, that all the ladies and gentlewomen had work enough to hold the queen up.

So when she might speak, she called ladies and gentlewomen to her, and said, 'Ye marvel, fair ladies, why I make this fare. Truly,' she said, 'it is for the sight of yonder knight that yonder standeth; wherefore I pray you all call him to me.'

When Sir Launcelot was brought to her, then she said to all the ladies, 'Through this man and me hath all this war been wrought, and the death of the most noblest knights of the world; for through our love that we have loved together is my most noble lord slain. Therefore, Sir Launcelot, wit thou well I am set in such a plight to get my soul health; and yet I trust through God's grace that after my death to have a sight of the blessed face of Christ, and at doomsday to sit on His right side, for as sinful as ever I was are saints in heaven. Therefore, Sir Launcelot, I require thee and beseech thee heartily, for all the love that ever was betwixt us, that thou never see me more in the visage; and I command thee, on God's behalf, that thou forsake my company, and to thy kingdom thou turn again, and keep well thy realm from war and wrack; for as well as I have loved thee, mine heart will not serve me to see thee, for through thee and me is the flower of kings and knights destroyed; therefore, Sir Launcelot, go to thy realm, and there take thee a wife, and live with her with joy and bliss; and I pray thee heartily, pray for me to Our Lord that I may amend my misliving.'

'Now, sweet madam,' said Sir Launcelot, 'would ye that I should turn again unto my country, and there to wed a lady? Nay, madam, wit you well that shall I never do, for I shall never be so false to you of that I have promised; but the same destiny that ye have taken you to, I will take me unto, for to please Jesu, and ever for you I cast me specially to pray.'

'If thou wilt do so,' said the queen, 'hold thy promise, but I may never believe but that thou wilt turn to the world again.'

'Well, madam,' said he, 'ye say as pleaseth you, yet wist you me never false of my promise, and God defend but I should forsake the world as ye have done. For in the quest of the Sangrail I had forsaken the vanities of the world had not your lord been. And if I had done so at that time, with my heart, will, and thought, I had passed all the knights that were in the Sangrail except Sir Galahad, my son. And therefore, lady, sithen ye have taken you to perfection, I must needs take me to perfection, of right. For I take record of God, in you I have had mine earthly joy; and if I had founden you now so disposed, I had cast me to have had you into mine own realm.

Chapter 10

'But sithen I find you thus disposed, I ensure you faithfully, I will ever take me to penance, and pray while my life lasteth, if that I may find any hermit, either gray or white, that will receive me. Wherefore, madam, I pray you kiss me and never no more.'

'Nay,' said the queen, 'that shall I never do, but abstain you from such works.' And they departed. But there was never so hard an hearted man but he would have wept to see the dolour that they made; for there was lamentation as they had been stungen with spears; and many times they swooned, and the ladies bare the queen to her chamber. And Sir

Launcelot awoke, and went and took his horse, and rode all that day and all night in a forest, weeping.

And at the last he was ware of an hermitage and a chapel stood betwixt two cliffs; and then he heard a little bell ring to mass, and thither he rode and alit, and tied his horse to the gate, and heard mass. And he that sang mass was the Bishop of Canterbury.

Both the Bishop and Sir Bedevere knew Sir Launcelot, and they spake together after mass. But when Sir Bedevere had told his tale all whole, Sir Launcelot's heart almost brast for sorrow, and Sir Launcelot threw his arms abroad, and said, 'Alas, who may trust this world.'

And then he kneeled down on his knee, and prayed the Bishop to shrive him and assoil him. And then he besought the Bishop that he might be his brother.

Then the Bishop said, 'I will gladly,' and there he put an habit upon Sir Launcelot, and there he served God day and night with prayers and fastings.

Thus the great host abode at Dover. And then

Sir Lionel took fifteen lords with him, and rode to London to seek Sir Launcelot; and there Sir Lionel was slain and many of his lords. Then Sir Bors de Ganis made the great host for to go home again; and Sir Bors, Sir Ector de Maris, Sir Blamor, Sir Bleoberis, with more other of Sir Launcelot's kin, took on them to ride all England overthwart and endlong, to seek Sir Launcelot. So Sir Bors by fortune rode so long till he came to the same chapel where Sir Launcelot was; and so Sir Bors heard a little bell knell, that rang to mass; and there he alit and heard mass. And when mass was done, the Bishop, Sir Launcelot, and Sir Bedevere, came to Sir Bors. And when Sir Bors saw Sir Launcelot in that manner clothing, then he prayed the Bishop that he might be in the same suit. And so there was an habit put upon him, and there he lived in prayers and fasting.

And within half a year, there was come Sir Galihud, Sir Galihodin, Sir Blamor, Sir Bleoberis, Sir Villiars, Sir Clarrus, and Sir Gahalantine. So all these seven noble knights there abode still. And when they saw Sir Launcelot had taken him to such perfection, they had no lust to depart, but took such an habit as he had. Thus they endured in great penance six year; and then Sir Launcelot took the habit of priesthood of the Bishop, and a twelvemonth he sang mass. And there was none of these other knights but they read in books, and holp for to sing mass, and rang bells, and did lowly all manner of service. And so their horses went where they would, for they took no regard of no worldly riches. For when they saw Sir Launcelot endure such penance, in prayers and fastings, they took no force what pain they endured, for to see the noblest knight of the world take such abstinence that he waxed full lean.

And thus upon a night, there came a vision to Sir Launcelot, and charged him, in remission of his sins, to haste him unto Almesbury: 'And by then thou come there, thou shalt find Queen Guenever dead. And therefore take thy fellows with thee, and purvey them of an horse bier, and fetch thou the corpse of her, and bury her by her husband, the noble King Arthur.' So this avision came to Sir Launcelot thrice in one night.

Chapter 11

Then Sir Launcelot rose up or day, and told the hermit.

'It were well done,' said the hermit, 'that ye made you ready, and that ye disobey not the avision.'

Then Sir Launcelot took his seven fellows with him, and on foot they yede from Glastonbury to Almesbury, the which is little more than thirty mile. And thither they came within two days, for they were weak and feeble to go. And when Sir Launcelot was come to Almesbury within the nunnery, Queen Guenever died but half an hour afore.

And the ladies told Sir Launcelot that Queen Guenever told them all or she passed, that Sir Launcelot had been priest near a twelvemonth, "And hither he cometh as fast as he may to fetch my corpse; and beside my lord, King Arthur, he shall bury me." Wherefore the queen said in hearing of them all, "I beseech Almighty God that I may never have power to see Sir Launcelot with my worldly eyen." 'And thus,' said all the ladies, 'was ever her prayer these two days, till she was dead.'

Then Sir Launcelot saw her visage, but he wept not greatly, but sighed. And so he did all the observance of the service himself, both the dirge, and on the morn he sang mass. And there was ordained an horse bier; and so with an hundred torches ever burning about the corpse of the queen, and ever Sir Launcelot with his seven fellows went about the horse bier, singing and reading many an holy orison, and frankincense upon the corpse incensed. Thus Sir Launcelot and his seven fellows went on foot from Almesbury unto Glastonbury.

And when they were come to the chapel and the hermitage, there she had a dirge, with great devotion. And on the morn the hermit that sometime was Bishop of Canterbury sang the mass of requiem with great devotion. And Sir Launcelot was the first that offered, and then all his eight fellows.

And then she was wrapped in cered cloth of Rennes, from the top to the toe, in thirtyfold; and after she was put in a web of lead, and then in a coffin of marble. And when she was put in the earth Sir Launcelot swooned, and lay long still, while the hermit came and awaked him, and said, 'Ye be to blame, for ye displease God with such manner of sorrow making.'

'Truly,' said Sir Launcelot, 'I trust I do not displease God, for He knoweth mine intent. For my sorrow was not, nor is not, for any rejoicing of sin, but my sorrow may never have end. For when I remember of her beauty, and of her noblesse, that was both with her king and with her, so when I saw his corpse and her corpse so lie together, truly mine heart would not serve to sustain my careful body. Also when I remember me how by my default, mine orgule and my pride, that they were both laid full low, that were peerless that ever was living of Christian people, wit you well,' said Sir Launcelot, 'this remembered, of their kindness and mine unkindness, sank so to mine heart, that I might not sustain myself.' So the French book maketh mention.

Chapter 12

Then Sir Launcelot never after ate but little meat, nor drank, till he was dead. For then he sickened more and more, and dried, and dwined away. For the Bishop nor none of his fellows might not make him to eat, and little he drank, that he was waxen by a cubit shorter than he was, that the people could not know him. For evermore, day and night, he prayed, but sometime he slumbered a broken sleep; ever he was lying grovelling on the tomb of King Arthur and Queen Guenever. And there was no comfort that the Bishop, nor Sir Bors, nor none of his fellows, could make him, it availed not.

So within six weeks after, Sir Launcelot fell sick, and lay in his bed; and then he sent for the Bishop that there was hermit, and all his true fellows. Then Sir Launcelot said with dreary steven, 'Sir

43

Bishop, I pray you give to me all my rites that longeth to a Christian man.'

'It shall not need you,' said the hermit and all his fellows, 'it is but heaviness of your blood, ye shall be well mended by the grace of God tomorn.'

'My fair lords,' said Sir Launcelot, 'wit you well my careful body will into the earth, I have warning more than now I will say; therefore give me my rites.'

So when he was houselled and eneled, and had all that a Christian man ought to have, he prayed the Bishop that his fellows might bear his body to Joyous Gard. Some men say it was Alnwick, and some men say it was Bamborough.

'Howbeit,' said Sir Launcelot, 'me repenteth sore, but I made mine avow sometime, that in Joyous Gard I would be buried. And because of breaking of mine avow, I pray you all, lead me thither.'

Then there was weeping and wringing of hands among his fellows. So at a season of the night they all went to their beds, for they all lay in one chamber. And so after midnight, against day, the Bishop that was hermit, as he lay in his bed asleep, he fell upon a great laughter. And therewithal the fellowship awoke, and come to the Bishop, and asked him what he ailed.

'Ah Jesu mercy,' said the Bishop, 'why did ye awake me? I was never in all my life so merry and so well at ease.'

'Wherefore?' said Sir Bors.

'Truly,' said the Bishop, 'here was Sir Launcelot with me with more angels than ever I saw men in one day. And I saw the angels heave up Sir Launcelot unto heaven, and the gates of heaven opened against him.'

'It is but dretching of swevens,' said Sir Bors, 'for I doubt not Sir Launcelot aileth nothing but good.'

'It may well be,' said the Bishop; 'go ye to his bed, and then shall ye prove the sooth.'

So when Sir Bors and his fellows came to his bed they found him stark dead, and he lay as he had smiled, and the sweetest savour about him that ever they felt. Then was there weeping and wringing of hands, and the greatest dole they made that ever made men.

And on the morn the Bishop did his mass of

requiem; and after, the Bishop and all the nine knights put Sir Launcelot in the same horse bier that Queen Guenever was laid in tofore that she was buried. And so the Bishop and they all together went with the body of Sir Launcelot daily, till they came to Joyous Gard; and ever they had an hundred torches burning about him. And so within fifteen days they came to Joyous Gard.

And there they laid his corpse in the body of the choir, and sang and read many psalters and prayers over him and about him. And ever his visage was laid open and naked, that all folks might behold him. For such was the custom in those days, that all men of worship should so lie with open visage till that they were buried.

And right thus as they were at their service, there came Sir Ector de Maris, that had seven year sought all England, Scotland, and Wales, seeking his brother, Sir Launcelot.

Chapter 13

HOW SIR ECTOR FOUND SIR LAUNCELOT HIS
BROTHER DEAD, AND HOW CONSTANTINE
REIGNED NEXT AFTER ARTHUR; AND OF THE
END OF THIS BOOK

And when Sir Ector heard such noise and light in the choir of Joyous Gard, he alit and put his horse from him, and came into the choir, and there he saw men sing, weep, and all they knew Sir Ector, but he knew not them.

Then went Sir Bors unto Sir Ector, and told him how there lay his brother, Sir Launcelot, dead; and then Sir Ector threw his shield, sword, and helm from him. And when he beheld Sir Launcelot's visage, he fell down in a swoon. And when he waked it were hard any tongue to tell the doleful complaints that he made for his brother.

'Ah Launcelot,' he said, 'thou were head of all Christian knights, and now I dare say,' said Sir Ector, 'thou Sir Launcelot, there thou liest, that thou were never matched of earthly knight's hand. And thou were the courteoust knight that ever bare shield. And thou were the truest friend to thy lover that ever bestrad horse. And thou were the truest lover of a sinful man that ever loved woman. And thou were the kindest man that ever struck with sword. And thou were the goodliest person that ever came among press of knights. And thou was the meekest man and the gentlest that ever ate in hall among ladies. And thou were the sternest knight to thy mortal foe that ever put spear in the rest.'

Then there was weeping and dolour out of measure. Thus they kept Sir Launcelot's corpse loft fifteen days, and then they buried it with great devotion.

And then at leisure they went all with the Bishop of Canterbury to his hermitage, and there they were together more than a month.

Then Sir Constantine, that was Sir Cador's son of Cornwall, was chosen king of England. And he was a full noble knight, and worshipfully he ruled this realm. And then this King Constantine sent for the Bishop of Canterbury, for he heard say where he was. And so he was restored unto his bishopric, and left that hermitage. And Sir Bedevere was there ever still hermit to his life's end.

Then Sir Bors de Ganis, Sir Ector de Maris, Sir Gahalantine, Sir Galihud, Sir Galihodin, Sir Blamor, Sir Bleoberis, Sir Villiars le Valiant, Sir Clarrus of Cleremont, all these knights drew them to their countries. Howbeit King Constantine would have had them with him, but they would not abide in this realm. And there they all lived in their countries as holy men.

And some English books maken mention that they went never out of England after the death of Sir Launcelot, but that was but favour of makers. For the French book maketh mention, and is authorised, that Sir Bors, Sir Ector, Sir Blamor, and Sir Bleoberis, went into the Holy Land thereas Jesu Christ was quick and dead, and anon as they had stablished their lands. For the book saith, so Sir Launcelot commanded them for to do, or ever he passed out of this world. And these four knights did many battles upon the miscreants or Turks. And there they died upon a Good Friday for God's sake.

PENGUIN 60s CLASSICS

PENGUIN 60s CLASSICS

HENRY JAMES · *The Lesson of the Master*
FRANZ KAFKA · *The Judgement*
THOMAS À KEMPIS · *Counsels on the Spiritual Life*
HEINRICH VON KLEIST · *The Marquise of O—*
LIVY · *Hannibal's Crossing of the Alps*
NICCOLÒ MACHIAVELLI · *The Art of War*
SIR THOMAS MALORY · *The Death of King Arthur*
GUY DE MAUPASSANT · *Boule de Suif*
FRIEDRICH NIETZSCHE · *Zarathustra's Discourses*
OVID · *Orpheus in the Underworld*
PLATO · *Phaedrus*
EDGAR ALLAN POE · *The Murders in the Rue Morgue*
ARTHUR RIMBAUD · *A Season in Hell*
JEAN-JACQUES ROUSSEAU · *Meditations of a Solitary Walker*
ROBERT LOUIS STEVENSON · *Dr Jekyll and Mr Hyde*
TACITUS · *Nero and the Burning of Rome*
HENRY DAVID THOREAU · *Civil Disobedience*
LEO TOLSTOY · *The Death of Ivan Ilyich*
IVAN TURGENEV · *Three Sketches from a Hunter's Album*
MARK TWAIN · *The Man That Corrupted Hadleyburg*
GIORGIO VASARI · *Lives of Three Renaissance Artists*
EDITH WHARTON · *Souls Belated*
WALT WHITMAN · *Song of Myself*
OSCAR WILDE · *The Portrait of Mr W. H.*

ANONYMOUS WORKS

Beowulf and Grendel
Gilgamesh and Enkidu
Tales of Cú Chulaind

Buddha's Teachings
Krishna's Dialogue on the Soul
Two Viking Romances